To Laura

Square Fish

An Imprint of Holtzbrinck Publishers

Library of Congress Cataloging-in-Publication Data
McCarty, Peter.
Hondo and Fabian / Peter McCarty.
Summary: Hondo the dog gets to go to the beach and play with his friend Fred, while Fabian the cat spends the day at home.
1. Dogs—Juvenile fiction. 2. Cats—Juvenile fiction.
[1. Dogs—Fiction. 2. Cats—Fiction. 3. Pets—Fiction.] I. Title.
PZ10.3.M12685 Ho 2002 [E]—dc21   2001001884

ISBN-10: 0-312-36747-3
ISBN-13: 978-0-312-36747-3

Originally published in the United States by Henry Holt and Company, LLC

First Square Fish Edition: June 2007

10 9 8 7 6 5 4 3 2 1

Hondo & Fabian

written and illustrated by

Peter McCarty

SQUARE
FISH

Henry Holt and Company

Fabian on the windowsill,
Hondo on the floor—
two sleepy pets
in their favorite places.

"Wake up, Hondo.

Time to go!"

Hondo will have an adventure.

Fabian will stay home.

Where is Hondo going,
riding in a car?

Hondo is going to the beach
to meet his friend Fred.

Fabian is going to

the living room

to play with the baby.

Two happy dogs

dive in the waves.

Fabian dives for the door.

Hondo has fun with Fred.

Fabian has fun too.

Now Hondo is getting hungry.

He wishes he could eat the fish.

Fabian is getting hungry too.
He wishes he could eat
the turkey sandwich.

At last Hondo comes home.

It's time for dinner!

Side by side Hondo and Fabian

eat their food.

Hondo and Fabian, full and fat—
in their favorite places once again.

"Good night, Hondo."
"Good night, Fabian."

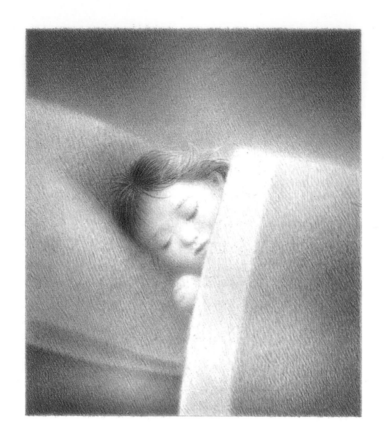

"Good night, baby!"

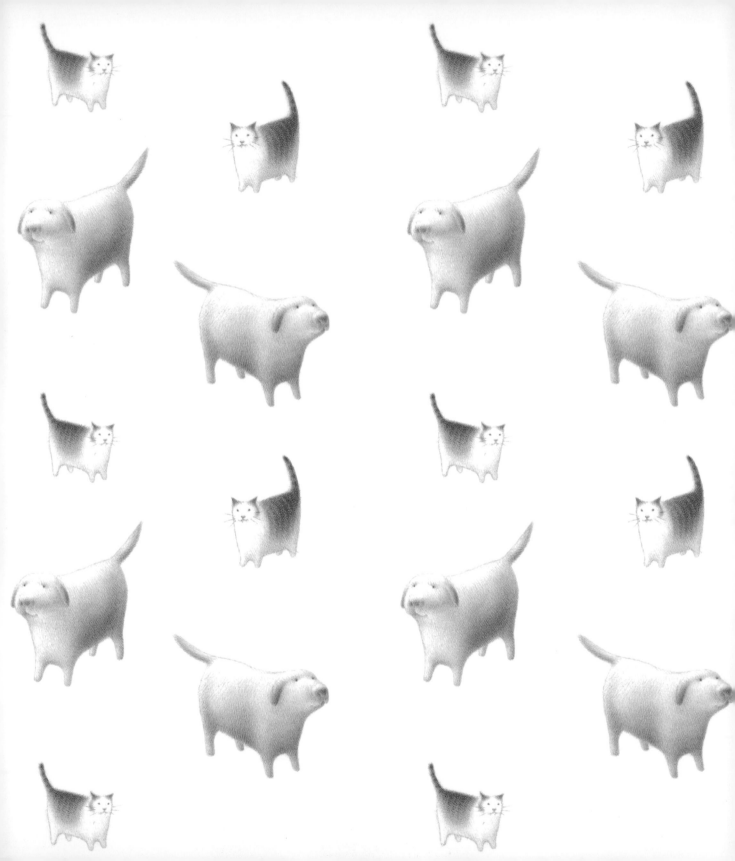